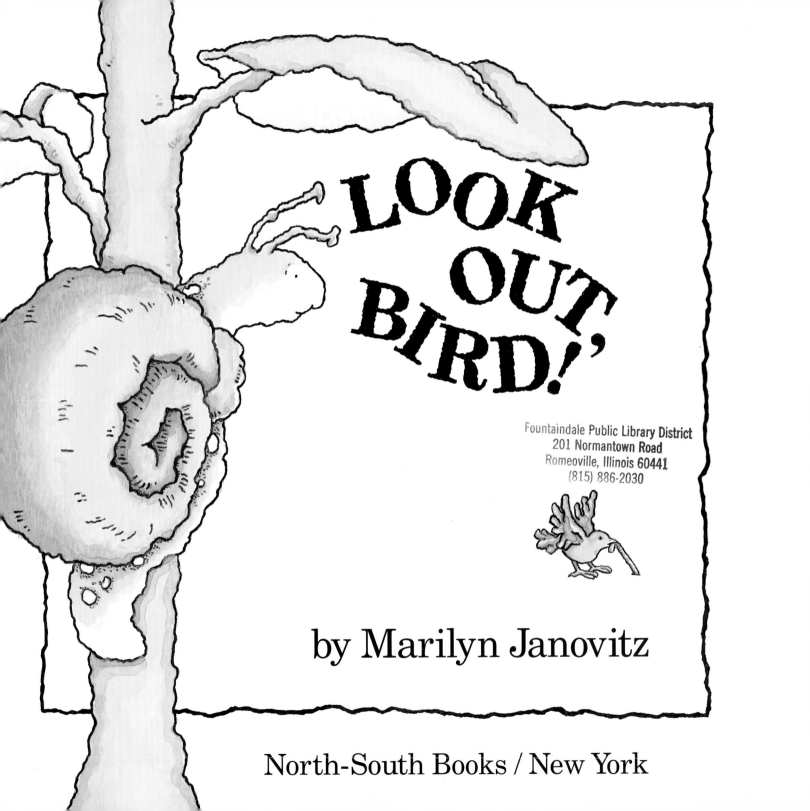

LOOK OUT, BIRD!'

by Marilyn Janovitz

North-South Books / New York

Published in the United States by North-South Books Inc., New York.

Published simultaneously in Great Britain, Canada,
Australia, and New Zealand in 1994 by North-South Books,
an imprint of Nord-Süd Verlag AG, Gossau Zürich, Switzerland.

Library of Congress Cataloging-in-Publication Data is available
A CIP catalogue record for this book is available from The British Library
ISBN 1-55858-249-5 (trade binding)
ISBN 1-55858-250-9 (library binding)

1 3 5 7 9 10 8 6 4 2
Printed in Belgium

The illustrations in this book were created
with pen-and-ink and watercolor

Book design and hand lettering
by Marilyn Janovitz

To
Mario

Snail slipped

and hit bird.

Bird flew

and frightened frog.

Frog jumped

and toppled turtle.

Turtle swam

and splashed salamander.

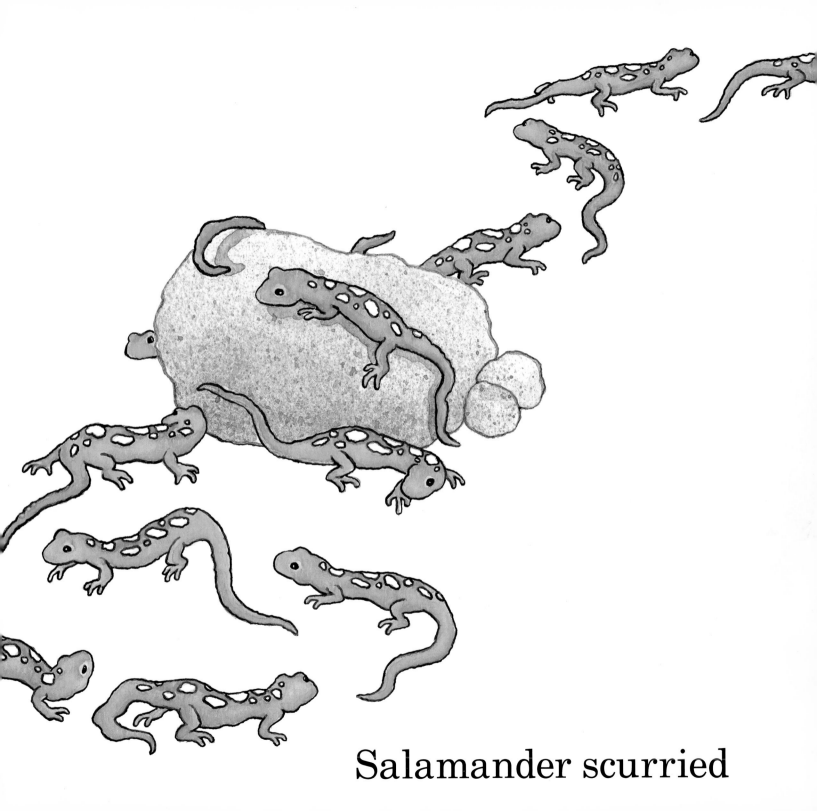

Salamander scurried

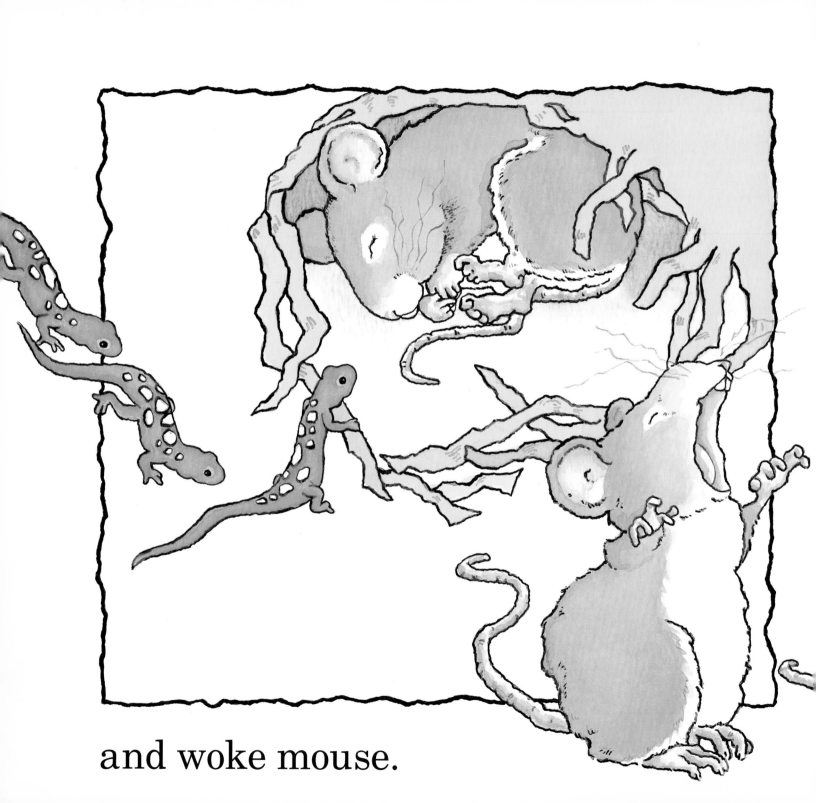

and woke mouse.

Mouse sniffed

and bothered bee.

Bee buzzed

and stung beaver.

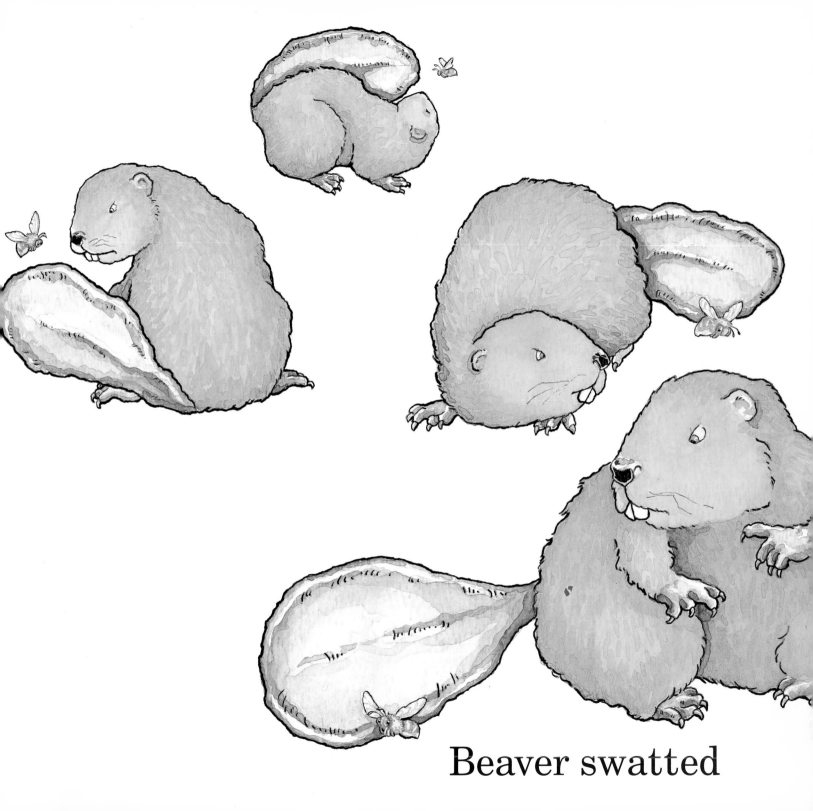

Beaver swatted

and slapped snake.

Snake slithered

and bumped beetle.

Beetle wobbled

and tickled toad.

Toad hopped

and knocked duck.

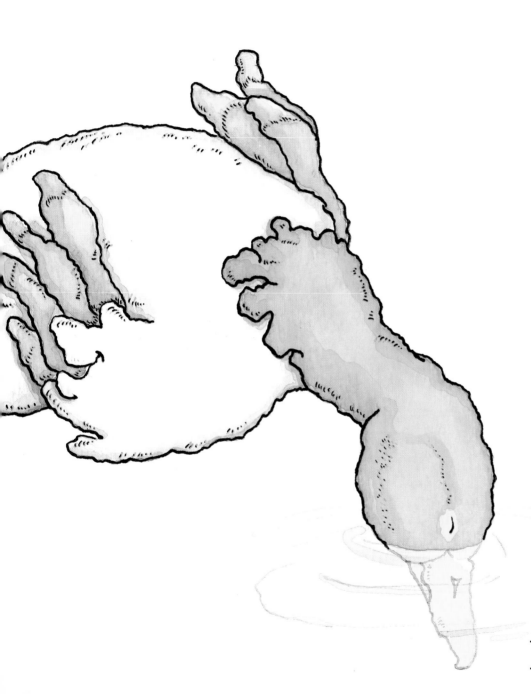

Duck dived

and flipped fish.

Fish flopped

and spattered moth.

Moth fluttered

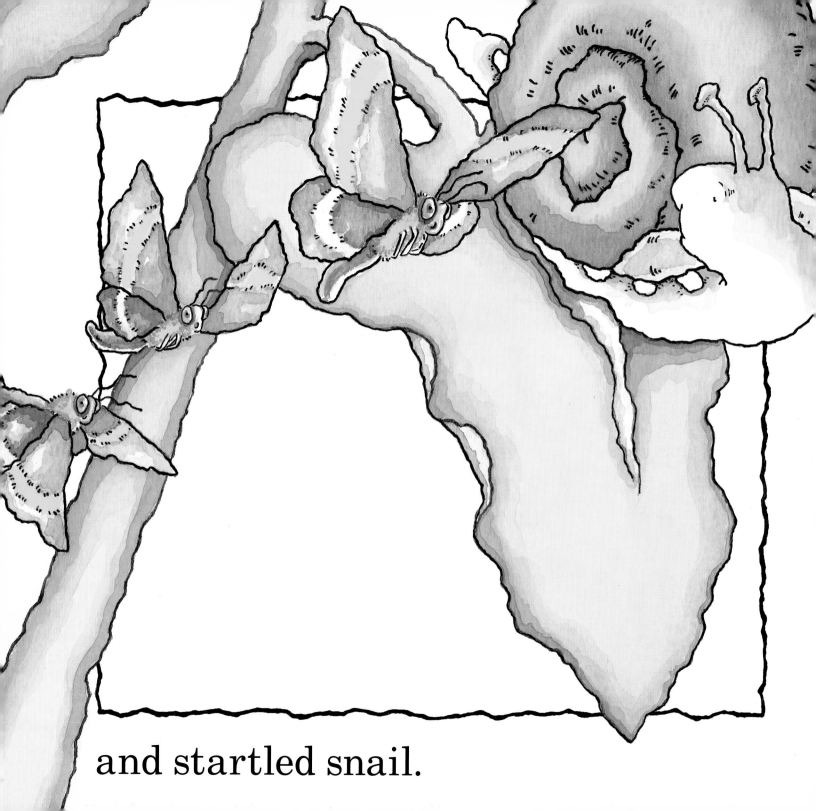

and startled snail.

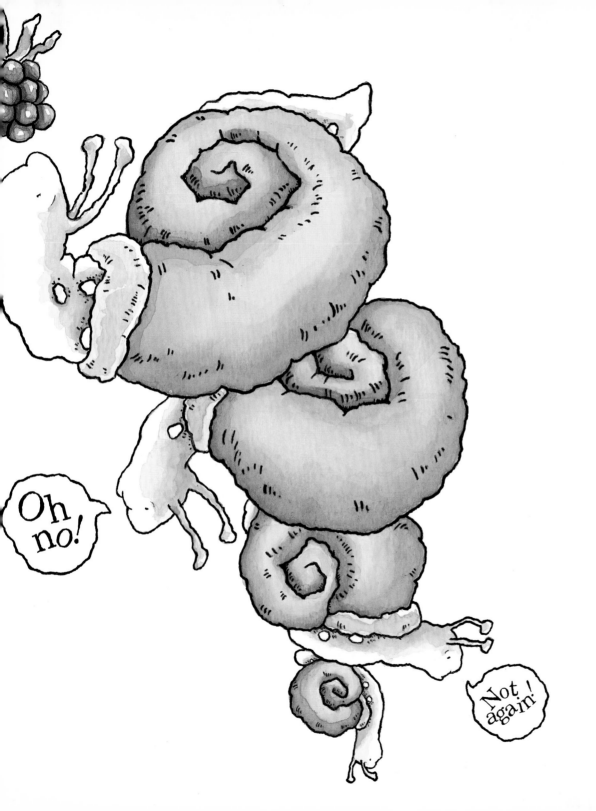